This Little Hippo
book belongs to

For Sally and Cuthbert.
S.H.

Scholastic Children's Books,
Commonwealth House, 1 – 19 New Oxford Street,
London WC1A 1NU
a division of Scholastic Ltd

London • New York • Toronto • Sydney • Auckland

First published in the UK by Little Hippo,
an imprint of Scholastic Ltd

Copyright © Scholastic Ltd 1997
Illustrations copyright © Sue Heap 1997

Based on an original idea by Alison Boyle

ISBN 0 590 19458 5

Printed and bound in China

2 4 6 8 10 9 7 5 3 1

The right of Sue Heap to be identified as the illustrator
of this work has been asserted by her in accordance
with the Copyright, Designs and Patents Act, 1988.

BUG IN A RUG

Sue Heap

Little Hippo

green bug

**red
rug**

grey towers

yellow flowers

white moon

black balloon

brown yak

purple mac

orange
plane

blue
train